Puppies Count

Kidsbooks®

Copyright © 2010 Kidsbooks, LLC
3535 West Peterson Avenue
Chicago, IL 60659

Story and illustrations by Mary Melcher.

Printed in China

031001011SZ

Visit us at **www.kidsbooks.com**®

One little
puppy playing
peek-a-boo!

Two little puppies find an old shoe.

Three naughty puppies
dig a big hole.

Four thirsty puppies
drink from a red bowl.

Five frisky
puppies chase
a fluffy cat.

Six silly puppies
hide Grandma's hat.

Seven noisy puppies
in a playful mood.

Eight hungry puppies running to their food.

Nine tired puppies having just been fed.

Ten little puppies
asleep in their bed.
Sweet dreams, little puppies.